Slick

Sara Cassidy

Orca currents

ORCA BOOK PUBLISHERS

Library and Archives Canada Cataloguing in Publication

Cassidy, Sara
Slick / written by Sara Cassidy.
(Orca currents)

Issued also in an electronic format.
ISBN 978-1-55469-353-5 (bound).--ISBN 978-1-55469-352-8 (pbk.)

I. Title. II. Series: Orca currents
PS8555.A7812S55 2010   JC813'.54   C2010-903583-6

First published in the United States, 2010
Library of Congress Control Number: 2010929085

Summary: Thirteen-year-old Liza gets involved in activism
and takes on the oil industry.

Mixed Sources
Cert no. SW-COC-001271
© 1996 FSC
FSC

*Orca Book Publishers is dedicated to preserving the environment and has printed this
book on paper certified by the Forest Stewardship Council.*

Orca Book Publishers gratefully acknowledges the support for its
publishing programs provided by the following agencies: the Government
of Canada through the Canada Book Fund and the Canada Council for the Arts,
and the Province of British Columbia through the BC Arts Council
and the Book Publishing Tax Credit.

Cover design by Teresa Bubela
Cover photography by Dreamstime

ORCA BOOK PUBLISHERS   ORCA BOOK PUBLISHERS
PO Box 5626, Stn. B   PO Box 468
Victoria, BC Canada   Custer, WA USA
v8R 6s4   98240-0468

www.orcabook.com
Printed and bound in Canada.

13 12 11 10 • 4 3 2 1

For Hazel

"Our cultural way is of respecting the land and living in harmony with it. Everything is in balance. All the animals, all the plants, even the rocks. There's no one thing that's more important than the other, and we're not any more important either. I don't think there's an understanding of that in the business world."

—Lynne Hill, Gitga'at Nation, British Columbia

Chapter One

"Could you get the map out of the glove compartment, Liza? You'll need the butter knife to pry it open. Stupid plastic latch," says Mom.

The butter knife is about a hundred years old. The handle is made of real cow bone that has yellowed over the years. The silver blade pops the glove box open perfectly. I find the map underneath a blue wool chauffeur's hat and a pair of cracked leather driving gloves.

"Here, give me those," Mom says, reaching out. "They'll help me focus." She wears the hat and gloves when she's cranky about driving.

Ever since Dad moved out, I sit up front beside my mom. It is perfect timing. The backseat was getting tight with my not-so-little-anymore brothers elbowing me and yelling to each other *through* my head. Mom tries to be environmentally friendly, which means we don't have a roomy SUV with TV screens. Our limpet-sized car starts on gas, then switches to electricity. It's called a hybrid.

"Like your hybrid running shoes," Mom said once to convince me this was cool.

"Like *one* of my runners," I'd said. "Where's the shoehorn to get us in?"

My mother *collects* shoehorns. She has one made from a seashell and an amazing one molded from paper. Mom also collects eggbeaters, irons, dice, globes, pictures of roads curving off into the distance, and many other things, like old butter knives. Objects are her business. She helps auction houses, museums and collectors figure out what their old things are worth. She can look at an old teacup and tell you who made it, who used it and how it made its way to your hands.

I like the color of our new car, I'll say that much. The color is Vixen Red, officially, but we call it Tomato Soup. It sure stands out, which means we no longer wander parking lots like dazed earthquake victims, looking for our small car.

I've been riding up front for a year, ever since Mom took us to Elk Lake and, in the middle of our nature walk, told us Dad was moving to England. Now when I go to Elk Lake, I look at the water and it's got that bad day in it. Somehow, though, it's still beautiful.

My parents' breakup is the same way. Dad's happier, Mom's happier, and the house is a lot calmer. Everything is better in lots of ways. Mom got busy after the panic was over. She reseeded our yard so the grass is lush for cartwheels, and she fixed up the house. She got the roof patched and the walls freshly painted. I do like the calm house. But that doesn't mean I'm not sad once in a while. Sometimes I feel as if I'm suffocating, I'm so sad.

I've learned what to do about the sadness. I get into bed and flip through my DIY books. DIY stands for Do It Yourself. It's about making cool stuff for really cheap or free, like by recycling or thrifting. *Thrifting* means shopping at thrift shops, which enviro-Mom totally supports. By the time I start making something, I feel fine again.

Last week, I made a bowl from an old music record in the stack Dad left behind. I put it on a cookie tray at two hundred degrees for five minutes, molded it over a metal dish and let it cool. I gave it to Leland to hold his arsenal of Playmobil swords and cannonballs. Now Silas, my older little brother, is begging me to make one for his compass collection.

Leland is six, energetic, and cuddly about once a month. He's cute though, especially when he's sleeping. Silas is cute too. Both my brothers have little noses and swarms of freckles. People say the three of us look like fairy children—whatever that means. Silas is really sensitive. He doesn't like other people to be sad or upset. He cries easily, but he also laughs easily. And he'll drop everything anytime to play with me.

"My butt's sore from all this driving," Silas calls out after a while.

"Yeah! My heinie's numb!" Leland shouts in agreement.

"My tush feels like it's on a porcupine," Mom says. Then she reaches under her and pulls out a hairbrush.

As we drive along, we start to make a list of words for *bum*. We get twenty-one! There's bum, bottom, behind, heinie, butt, derriere, buns, buttocks, rear end, fanny, cheeks, posterior, rear, rump, seat, gluteus maximus, backside, keister, haunches, tush and can. There is also a word that also means donkey. This brings our list to twenty-two, even though we're not allowed to say all the words. Mom says we're not allowed to curse until we're eighteen, which is totally ridiculous. She only lets us swear if we're singing along to the Black Eyed Peas.

The car windows are open, and Silas is chanting *gluteus maximus* with a stuffy English accent. "Gluteus maximus, gluteus maximus," he warbles.

"Has anyone seen my gluteus maximus?" We're screaming with laughter. A man and his pug-faced dog stare as we drive by. Take a picture, sir. Take a picture of me and my awesome family.

Then we pull up in front of Mom's new boyfriend's house.

I get out of the front seat and climb over Leland's lap into the cramped backseat. Mom checks her teeth for green bits or whatever in the rearview mirror. Then she looks up and waves big to *him* as he locks up his house.

He gets into the front seat. "Hi, Laura! Hi, kids!" he says, overfriendly and not waiting for an answer. I don't even want to say his name. I hate him.

I totally, absolutely, completely, really, truly hate him.

Chapter Two

"Come on, Liza, he's not *that* bad. It's not like he's wanted by the police." Olive, my best friend, is always urging me to be less emotional. Miss Level-Headed lives two doors down in a super organized house with polished floors and pillowy reading nooks. They even have a meditation room and a grand piano no one ever plays. Olive gets up at seven every morning to start her daily chores. This includes feeding the purebred Abyssinian cat Horus and making her parents' bed. Yes, Olive makes her parents' bed. But *they* make *hers*. "It's a loving exchange of labor," her mom once explained.

"Olive, he's stupid. He's got zits. He's just creepy," I shout as we steer our scooters to the grocery store. Mom has sent us to get black beans and salsa for the quesadillas she's making for supper. Saturday is international night at our house. Sometimes we eat Moroccan, sometimes Greek or Thai. Tonight it's Mexican.

Emergency grocery trips used to be Dad's job. To reward me for doing them, Mom lets me get anything I want, as long as it's healthy. Today I'm buying mini-marshmallows. Okay, mini-marshmallows aren't healthy, but I don't plan to eat them. This morning I made marshmallow shooters out of PVC piping.

Now, an afternoon spent mounting invasions, blockades, blitzkriegs and sneak attacks is totally healthy.

"My dad thinks you're scared that he's going to take your mom away," Olive says.

"That would be so cool!" I say. "Silas, Leland and I could have the house to ourselves, eat ice cream straight out of the tub, keep goats—"

"Yeah, right, Pippi Longstocking." Olive rolls her eyes and smiles.

I love it when she smiles. It's like she smiles twice, like she's happy to be happy. Olive's dad is a psychiatrist. He makes his living figuring out why people feel the way they do, kind of a detective of the mind. It's rubbing off on Olive.

"Your dad left." Olive is serious again. "Maybe you're afraid your mom's going to leave."

It hurts like hell when Olive says this. I mean it hurts like *heck*. I'm not allowed to say *hell*. But *hell* is sharper than *heck*—meaner. It fits the cutting feeling I have just thinking about my mom leaving.

"Or you still want your dad to come back, which can't happen if this guy's in the picture—"

"Olive, I've told you, my parents are not getting back together. This isn't some happily-ever-after Disney movie—"

"But if you actually start to like Robert—"

"His name is Slick," I remind her. I've named him Slick, as in oil slick, because he works for an oil company. And because he's greasy.

"Okay, *Slick*—" Olive smirks. "If you start to like Slick, you'd be saying that, yes, things have changed. Life is never going to return to what it was."

"He's smarmy and ugly, and his feet turn out when he walks," I say. "And he's always happy, or fake happy.

There's nothing complicated about it. I hate him."

I hold back from saying I hate her too. At that moment, I do hate Olive. And her dad.

But I'm saved from this stupid discussion because we arrive at the supermarket. The parking lot is crazy lively. It's decorated with balloons, and a not-terrible band is playing on a makeshift stage.

"Customer appreciation day," explains an employee as she hands us slabs of white cake on flimsy paper plates. "A day that *we* appreciate *you,* our customers."

"Wow," Olive and I say in unison. It is like being anointed as royal customers.

We perch on one of those concrete slugs that divide up parking lots. With plates balanced on our knees, we watch the band. The lead singer is a dude my mom's age with strings of hair dangling from the shores of a bald spot. He shakes his head, sending a shower of sweat our way.

"Ugh! It landed in your cake!" I cry in mock horror. With queenly poise, Olive delicately works her plastic fork around the area we call the Rock Star Sweat Spot. That gets us laughing until we lean against each other, gasping for breath.

Chapter Three

"*Za*? That's a word?" Mom looks doubtful, one shaggy eyebrow raised.

"Za. As in piz-za," I say. "A round thing covered with melted cheese?"

"I'll look it up! I'll look it up!" Silas yells. He starts thumbing the Scrabble dictionary as he jumps on my mom's double bed.

"More tea, dear ladies?" Leland asks, bowing with a tea towel over one arm.

When Mom and I play Scrabble, Silas is Dictionary Boy and Leland is Tea Boy. Leland pours half the tea onto the table rather than in our cups, but at least Mom and I get to play.

"With the *z* on triple letter score for thirty points," I sweetly point out.

"I know, I know."

"But I count the thirty points twice because, going down, the *z* turns your *it* into *zit*. Let's see now, thirty plus thirty…"

"Okay, *okay*." Mom laughs.

"Aren't you impressed by my intelligence?"

"No," Mom says. "I'm not. Because the very first time I looked at wrinkled, red-faced, screaming you, I thought, 'Goodness, *this* is a smart one.'"

"Yeah, right," I mumble.

"Yeah. *Right*." Mom watches me. Finally I nod, and she's satisfied that I believe her.

"Hello?" a voice calls from downstairs. It's Rachael, the boys' viola-playing, hot-chocolate-making babysitter. Usually I babysit the boys, but Mom's been going out so much lately, I'm fed up with looking after them.

"We'll be right down!" Mom sings. "If I can still walk. Liza has crushed me at Scrabble again.

"You know," she tells me, "it fills me with joy when my children do something better than I can." Then she looks at the clock by the bed, cries, "Oh, goodness!" and yanks her closet door open. "Clean up the game, will you? I've got to dress."

Minutes later, Slick is at the door. Silas and Leland pelt him with marshmallows, which is great. I urge them on, "Harder! Harder!" Slick just laughs, scoops up the marshmallows and throws them back. What a nerd.

"Hi, Liza," he says, his smile smeared on like veneer.

"Yeah," I say, checking out his ugly shoes. Judging by the sour, deadly smell, he has recently polished them.

"I brought you something," he says. He reaches into a plastic bag and pulls out five spools of embroidery thread and an instruction book for making friendship bracelets. "I know you like crafts."

"Hm," I grunt. I won't be making *him* a friendship bracelet.

"And I found this cheese grater for your mom. It's from the late 1800s, Southern US." Slick pulls the metal contraption from his bag. "You put a cube of cheese in here, turn this crank and, *wham-o*, the stuff falls like snow."

Wham-o?

Slick reaches into his bag again. "Boys!" he says. "Here are a couple of twirlers. An old guy in my neighbor-hood carves them from maple."

Silas and Leland are easily bought. Thrilled, they spin the wooden propellers into the air and try to catch them. I can't wait to get my hands on one—once Slick and my mom have left.

"Say *thank you*, Liza," Mom says, coming down the stairs. She's in a blue dress I've never seen before. It's shorter than her other dresses. Her hair is in a bun so elegant it whispers *chignon*, and she's wearing lipstick. Mom *never* wears lipstick.

"I *did* say thank you," I blurt, hurrying into my room. Why does she make herself look so nice for him? She doesn't even look like a mom. I take my copy of *Pippi Longstocking* down from my bookshelf and start to read. Not much later, Mom calls from the front door, "Bye, Liza! I love you!"

Through my bedroom window, I watch her and Slick walk toward town. I can tell from the back that my mom's laughing, and—ugh—they're holding hands.

Chapter Four

It's the first day of October. The principal announces she's turned on the furnace for the first time this year. But the school still feels chilly because I have a cold. It's a relief when the custodian wheels in the video player. Our social-studies teacher, Ms. Catalla, turns off the lights, and I get to slump on my desk and just watch.

We're learning about Central America, the squiggle of land between North and South America. The film is about kids in Guatemala who live in houses of sticks lashed together with vines. The roofs are made with tree branches or sheets of rippled metal. The people in the film are called Maya. They lived in Guatemala long before the Europeans, like the Coast Salish people around here or the Navajo in the US.

"Mayans have a long history, strong customs and a deep relationship with the land," sing-songs the narrator. "In ancient times they built pyramids and discovered the concept of zero at the same time it was discovered in India. They invented a calendar more accurate than ours and created the only full written language in this part of the world.

"But ever since the Spanish *conquistadores* arrived—nearly five hundred years ago—the Mayans have been treated brutally. Still, they've held on to their language, their food, religion and colorful weaving. Nearly half of Guatemalans are pure Mayan; another twenty percent share Spanish-Mayan heritage."

The film shows that they mostly grow corn, beans and coffee. The kids eat black beans and corn tortillas that their moms shape with their hands and cook over an open fire. Chicken is a treat for them. One kid tells the camera about a storm that ripped the metal roof off his house and landed on a chicken in the yard, killing it. "I heard the crash in the night." She laughs. "The sound of chicken soup!"

Even though they're poor and wear torn clothes and no shoes, the kids still laugh. Poverty isn't as simple as I thought. Some things about their lives are pretty cool, in fact. In the film, everyone in the town bathes in the same river, upstream from where the women wash clothes, which is upstream from where the farm animals drink. And everyone makes what they need. They build beds using branches they cut from the jungle. Kids as young as Leland use machetes to get firewood.

Near the end of the film, the kids are playing soccer with a paper bag they'd stuffed with leaves. I watch closely, so I can make one myself. Everyone's happy: the kids shout, birds caw in the nearby jungle. I am just thinking that their life is pretty great when, all of a sudden, a kid grabs the ball and everyone scurries to the side of the road.

A massive eighteen-wheeler barrels along the narrow dirt road, raising huge clouds of dust and spewing iodine-colored blooms of exhaust. The noise drowns out every other sound. The kids shut their eyes tight. They lift their T-shirts to their mouths to keep out the dust. Some clap their hands over their ears.

Once the truck passes, the kids slowly lower their hands from their faces. But then another truck bullies through. The side of the truck reads *Argenta Oil*. It's a name I know, but how?

Then it comes to me. *That's the company that Slick works for!*

"Elbows off the table, Liza. Silas, please chew with your mouth shut." Mom rolls her eyes at Slick, who winks at her. Mom doesn't usually care about our manners. Our house is totally clean too, cleaner than I've ever seen it. She's changing herself for him, changing *us*.

"So, Liza, how was school today?" Slick asks.

"How was *work* today?" I ask back.

"Boring," Slick says. "A meeting, then a meeting about that meeting, then a meeting about those two meetings." Silas and Leland giggle. Mom laughs too.

"I'm having dessert in my room," I announce, sliding off my chair. I can't take him anymore.

"Liza!" Mom calls, but I'm gone. She doesn't come after me.

For a while I throw a ball against my bedroom wall, over and over. It makes smudge marks on the wall. The marks remind me of that dirty landscape in the film, and I get angrier.

I get a paper bag and stuff it with newspaper. It's pretty difficult to make it round. I have to make cuts in a few places and bind it with masking tape. By the time I've made a soccer ball, I'm feeling better. I hear Mom say goodbye to Slick.

A few minutes later she comes into my room and sits on the end of my bed.

"Liza, it's natural for you to dislike Robert," she says. "You're worried he'll hurt me or take me away."

"I don't dislike him, Mom. I *hate* him. There's a difference."

"Oh, come on, Liza! He's a very nice man. But, sweetie, you have to know that no one, *no one*, will ever separate me from you or water down my love for you. That is impossible. My love for you only grows. Which is mathematically difficult, because it's already infinite. Can something infinite get bigger?"

Mom hugs me. I hug her back and cry. It's warm in her arms. Over her shoulder, I see the smudges on the wall. They are like a message of bad news.

I start to wonder, if she really loves me and knows how much I hate Slick, why does she keep dating him?

Chapter Five

Ms. Catalla lets me stay in at lunch to watch the documentary again while she marks homework at her desk.

"Why are you so interested in Guatemala?" she asks. Ms. Catalla reminds me of a sparrow. She's small and quick. She grew up in Colombia and speaks with a Spanish accent.

"I'm interested in how people who are poor can be happy," I lie. I glance at the sculpture of three monkeys on Ms. Catalla's desk. One has its hands over its eyes, another its hands over its ears, and a third covers its mouth. "And…and…," I stammer.

"Yes?"

"And those trucks that drive through when the kids are playing soccer. It's rude! I want to know about those trucks. How often do they rip through that town? Does the company make amends?"

"That's easy to research, Liza," Ms. Catalla says. I can tell she's really listening. "What do you think those trucks are doing?"

"Well, it looks like they're polluting," I say. "I bet the company pulled oil out of the ground near where those kids live. And they sell it for lots of money. The president of the company probably lives in a mansion. Those kids can't even afford a decent soccer ball."

"Those are good points, Liza."

"Argenta Oil's head office is downtown, you know," I say.

"I didn't know that," Ms. Catalla says. "How did you know?"

"I've seen it," I say. I glance at the monkeys and feel guilty for lying. "Actually, I know someone who works there. Or rather, I *hate* someone who works there."

"Is that why you're interested?

"I want to do something for those kids," I answer.

"Out of the goodness of your heart?" she asks. "Not out of revenge against this person you don't like?"

"Yes," I say. But Ms. Catalla has a point. Do I just want to dig up dirt on Slick? I think about it for a minute. No, it doesn't matter how I feel about Slick. Now that I know those kids are getting choked out of their games, I have to see if I can help.

Righting a wrong is the priority. Exposing Slick's evil company will just be a convenient bonus. I look over at Ms. Catalla's monkeys again. She follows my gaze.

"Mizaru," she says, patting the monkey with its hands over its eyes. "He sees no evil." Ms. Catalla strokes the one covering its ears. "Kikazaru. He hears no evil." Ms. Catalla puts her hand over her mouth, muffling her voice. "And Iwazaru speaks no evil. In Japan, these monkeys are a reminder to be of good mind, good speech and good action. Here in North America, they've come to represent people who pretend nothing bad is going on."

"Well, I don't want to be like that," I say.

After school, Olive and I borrow my mother's laptop. Ms. Catalla said I could research Argenta Oil's work in Guatemala for my next social-studies project. Olive takes a research class at her school and has agreed to help me.

We google *Argenta Oil Guatemala* to start. The first site we find is Argenta Oil's company site. It's about how wonderful the company is and how happy they are to have oil rights in Guatemala.

"What was the town in the documentary called?" Olive asks.

"Las Angelitas," I say.

We google *Las Angelitas Argenta Oil.* Nothing. "Don't worry," Olive says. "Research is mostly dead ends. Research. Like rewind, redo. You search over and over. Let's check out the town on Google Earth."

Pretty soon we are bearing down on the town, so close we can see the patchwork of steel roofs in the leafy jungle. I look for kids playing soccer. Okay, we're not *that* close.

The town is in the region of Riviera Selequa. We google *Argenta Oil Riviera Selequa*, and bingo!

"Wow," Olive mutters. "We've caught a big fish!"

We're on the website of Oilwatch, a citizens' group dedicated to "Uncovering the Eco-Crimes of the Oil Industry." The website says that farmers who live along Selequa River are taking Argenta Oil to court.

"They drilled on our land and made a mess," reports a farmer. She says the company's drilling killed animals, broke fences and polluted wells. "They must pay for repairs."

The website says the farmers have waited two years. Argenta should have paid up a long time ago.

"So, he *is* wanted by the police, Olive!"

At that moment, Mom walks in. "There you are."

She has had her hair cut. It looks nice. But there is something else... What?

"*Mom*, did you get your *eyebrows* done? You swore you'd never pluck! What happened to 'My shaggy, bushy, wooly, fuzzy, furry, fluffy, rugged, scraggy, tufted, bristly brows'?" This is a ditty she sings. "Or, 'So what if I'm wild? Better than mild!'"

"Liza, a person can change her mind, you know," says Mom.

"Changing ideas is different from changing *ideals*, Mom," I sputter.

Olive elbows me. I'm not sure if this means "Good one!" or "Be nice!"

"I'm going to a movie," Mom says. "Rachael's downstairs."

"Why don't you watch a movie here?" I ask. She and I often curled up together to watch a DVD.

"I'm going with Robert, sweetie. I'll be back to kiss you goodnight. Look, you guys can watch a bit of TV. Okay? Even though it's a school night. I'll tell Rachael—"

"Yeah, sure," I pout. "Have a good time with your boy-felon—"

"My what?"

"Boy-felon. Your boyfriend's company bullies poor farmers."

"What are you talking about?" Mom asks.

I hand her the laptop. "Read it and weep," I say sourly. "Isn't Guatemala where your fair-trade, organic, bird-friendly coffee comes from?"

"Hello?" It's Slick, calling from the door.

"I'll be there in a minute," Mom calls absently. She continues to read, furrowing those nicely shaped brows. Finally, she hands the computer back.

"I've got to go," she says. "We'll talk about this later."

After a little more research, Olive and I make a mini air horn with a film canister, a straw and a balloon. We cut a hole in the bottom of the canister and slide the straw into it. Then we cut a smaller hole in the side of the canister to blow into. We stretch a piece of balloon over the top and snap the lid on. Get ready for 120 decibels!

Later, we brush glow-in-the-dark paint onto the propellers that Slick gave the boys. We stand on the back deck and send them spinning into the yard. They are a dizzy glow in the night air. Beautiful! I imagine one sailing all the way to Guatemala and being caught by a child in Las Angelitas.

Chapter Six

For breakfast, I make a huge pot of hot chocolate, adding half a teaspoon of cinnamon and a pinch of nutmeg. I'm using Rachael's recipe. Silas and I play chess while we drink from our mugs. Leland spins a Ninja Turtle in the new cheese grater. Mom is fixated on the newspaper.

"Incredible," she says. "A curator's nightmare! Check this out: the Cleveland Museum thought they had a real hair from Amelia Earhart's head. But all these years, it was a piece of thread!"

"Who's Amelia Earhart?" Leland asks, spinning his Ninja Turtle more slowly.

"A famous aviator. Well, *aviatrix* is what they called the women. There were many female pilots during the world wars. When the wars ended, a few managed to keep flying. They ran deliveries, taught at flight schools and some did stunts at fairs."

"Wing walking," says Silas, who reads every nonfiction book that comes under his radar. "Barnstorming. One woman danced the Charleston on the wing of a plane at 2,200 feet."

"That's right!" Mom says. "Amelia Earhart was the first woman to fly solo across the Atlantic. Then she tried to fly around the world. But she disappeared over the Pacific Ocean. Seventy-five years ago. She was never found."

"But someone had one of her hairs?" I ask.

"They thought they did. Before setting off around the world, Amelia was a guest of President Roosevelt's. A maid at the White House plucked a hair from the pillowcase Amelia had slept on, as a souvenir. It eventually ended up in the museum's collection. But they just ran a DNA test to see if it matched some bones recently found on a Pacific Ocean island. All these years, and it was just a thread!"

"She's good at vanishing!" Leland exclaims.

"I'll say!" Mom laughs and then looks at the clock. "Race time!" She upends all five of our egg timers. We leap from the table, brush our teeth, get our shoes and jackets and backpacks. We're out the door before the last grains of sand fall to the bottom of the crow-shaped, African Blackwood egg timer. It's our favorite, since it's the slowest, giving us a full fifteen seconds extra.

Ms. Catalla isn't surprised by what Olive and I discovered online.

"It would be hard to find an oil company that isn't running over people's toes," she says. "Still, you need to find out whether Argenta is acting in bad faith. Do they know they're doing wrong? And, if they are acting in bad faith, what will you do? There is a common belief that if you know something bad is happening and you do nothing to stop it, you're part of the problem."

"But what can I do?" I say, trying not to whine. "I'm not a lawyer. I don't live in Guatemala…"

"But you *are* someone," Ms. Catalla urges gently.

"I'm a kid. A teenager. A student." I feel stronger by the second. "I'm Canadian. So is Argenta Oil. And I've been owed money. It sucks."

Mom drives us to the beach for a picnic supper. It's a cool evening. We pack sweaters and blankets. I also bring a cookie sheet so I can test for rattlebacks, also called wobblestones or Celtic stones.

Rattlebacks are ancient toys that can be made from pretty much anything. They're shaped like a twisted kayak and fit easily in one hand. You place them on a flat surface and spin them. In one direction, they spin as you'd expect, eventually slowing to a stop. But when you spin them in the other direction, they spin for a while, slow down, start to wobble, then, *on their own*, reverse in the other direction for a little spin! It's kind of eerie. I have a rattleback collection. Some are carved from wood, some are clay. I have one that is just a telephone receiver that happened to be weighted right, and one I made with a stick of gum in its foil, bent into shape. Five of the rattlebacks in my collection are stones I found on the beach.

After our supper of salmon sandwiches, I look for rocks that are long and curve upward at both ends. Mom stokes the fire with a piece of driftwood. Then she throws the stick toward two seagulls thrusting their beaks into the picnic basket. "Shoo! That's our dessert!" Silas and Leland are across the beach, building a driftwood fort.

After a while, Mom speaks. "So Argenta Oil's no angel."

"That's right," I agree.

"But how on earth did you find out? Why were you digging around?"

"Mom, that doesn't matter," I say. "The point is, the company your boyfriend works for is evil."

"That's a little extreme, Liza."

"What's extreme is how poor the Maya are. They've been robbed, Mom, big-time," I say. "Ooh! Got one!" We watch as my stone spins, slows, wobbles, then changes direction.

"Good one!" Mom cheers before turning serious again. "Liza, Robert is a good person. He has a good heart."

"Well, if someone works for an evil—okay, bad—company, doesn't that make *them* bad?"

"Maybe he doesn't know," says Mom. "Like that museum in Cleveland—they didn't mean to dupe anyone by displaying that hair. Or imagine one of the auction houses is selling stolen goods, but I don't know it. I appraise the goods and help the auction house sell them. Am I a thief too?"

"No. Of course not."

"Robert needs a job—he's got a house and car to pay for," Mom argues.

"Anyway, probably every company has a bad record somewhere. No one's perfect, Liza."

"Mom, stealing from poor people is a long way from 'not perfect.' Couldn't Slick talk to his bosses? Get them to pay up?"

"*Robert* would probably be fired," Mom shrugs. "Or moved to a lesser position."

"For telling the truth? So he works at a place where he can't say what he wants?" I had a vision of Slick, crouched like a monkey, a hand over his smile.

Just then we hear Silas scream, "Leland's in the water! Leland's in the water!'

Mom and I leap up, but a woman walking her dog near the boys wades into the water and grabs Leland before we can get there. He is sobbing while the woman soothes him, "There, there, it's all right."

Mom is crying. "Thank you! Oh, thank you. What if you hadn't been there? He would have been lost!"

"But I *was* there," the woman says, calmly putting an arm around Mom. She is older than Mom and nicely dressed in a long coat and white leather boots. "Everything's fine."

"You're wet," Mom says to her. "Come, get warmed up by the fire. We'll gather our things and drive you home."

"Thank you," says the woman. "And thank you!" she says cheerfully to a chattering Leland. "I wondered how cold the water was, and now I know!"

"I'd really like to make it up to you," Mom says as we drop the woman off.

"Don't worry about that," says the woman. "Really. It's just nice to see a family that's so close."

"I'm going to report her to the police!" Mom announces as we pull out of the woman's driveway. "For heroism!"

"No kidding! She was old!" Silas says. "And she just jumped into the freezing water, got her fancy boots wet."

"Yeah," I agree, darting a look at Mom. "It was about doing the right thing, not about *things*, like a nice house and car."

"What are you talking about?" Silas asks, perplexed.

"It's just something between me and Liza, honey," Mom says firmly. "A subject we're going to give a rest right now. Okay, Liza?"

"Okay," I mutter. "But—"

"That woman was a mermaid," Leland sighs. He is drifting off to sleep. "I'd walk the plank for her."

Chapter Seven

From: LittleLizaJane@whoohoo.com
To: OilWatch@geemail.com

Dear OilWatch,
I'd like to help make Argenta Oil pay for drilling on Mayan land. I'm a grade 7 student in Victoria, where the company has its head office.

I watched a documentary about the Maya of the Ixcán, where Argenta Oil trucks plow through the kids' soccer games, choking the air with dust and exhaust.

Could you send me info about the court case and scummy Argenta Oil? I'm also researching the company for a school project.

Thank you,

Liza Maybird

From: OilWatch@geemail.com
To: LittleLizaJane@whoohoo.com

Dear Liza,

Totally cool to hear from you. You're right: Argenta Oil is scummy!

Our organization keeps track of oil companies in Central America. We alert politicians and the media—newspapers, radio and TV stations, bloggers—when people or the land get hurt. We also raise money to help with legal costs.

In community elections, where even seven-year-olds vote, over 90 percent of Mayans vote against oil companies using their land. But the government of Guatemala doesn't give two pennies about what the Maya want. Activists say the government kidnaps and even kills Mayans who speak out against oil companies.

When drilling, oil companies can ruin cropland, knock over farm buildings, pollute…The company is supposed to pay compensation for the damage. In Guatemala, they have ninety days to pay.

Fifty Guatemalan farmers have waited two years for $500,000 in compensation from Argenta. That may sound like a lot, but compared to what Argenta makes…let's just say that last year, the head of Argenta gave himself a $2 million bonus!

We want oil companies to leave the Maya people alone. Compensation is a small issue, but this campaign will introduce the bigger ones.

Attached is more info. We'd love your help!
In solidarity,
Jamaica Chappell

From: LittleLizaJane@whoohoo.com
To: OilWatch@geemail.com

Dear Jamaica,
Thanks for writing back so quickly and taking
me seriously.
    Two questions:
    1. Is Argenta Oil breaking the law?
    2. What's the bonus for?
    Cheers,
    Liza

From: OilWatch@geemail.com
To: LittleLizaJane@whoohoo.com

Liza!
Good questions!

1: If you held Argenta Oil to Canadian standards, they are breaking the law. Argenta pays its Guatemalan workers one-tenth of what it pays its workers in Canada. In Canada, Argenta Oil helps its workers if they get injured on the job. Not in Guatemala. In Canada, Argenta pays into a pension plan. Not in Guatemala. In Canada, they provide safety equipment. Not in Guatemala. In Canada, they follow environmental protection laws. Not in Guatemala.

In Guatemala, Argenta has to obey Guatemalan laws—and for the most part they do. But those laws are weak. In Guatemala, they don't have to take their workers or the Earth seriously. They make more money that way.

2: A bonus is usually a reward for good work. Sometimes it's a payout when a company's made a lot of money.

I've always wanted to visit Victoria. It's so close to Seattle, which is where I live.

In peace,

Jamaica

From: LittleLizaJane@whoohoo.com
To: OilWatch@geemail.com

Hi Jamaica,
I definitely want to help with the campaign.
> But I have no idea where to start.
> TTYS,
> Liza
> P.S. I've always wanted to see Seattle.

From: OilWatch@geemail.com
To: LittleLizaJane@whoohoo.com

Hi Liza,
If you ever do visit Seattle, come see us at OilWatch.

There's a lot you can do to pressure Argenta. Your school project is a great start. Research and knowledge, along with compassion and justice, are the only true weapons.

You could write an article for your local newspaper. Write to the president of Argenta, and send copies of your letter to local newspapers, radio stations and politicans.

Draw up a petition: write at the top of a piece of paper something like: *We demand that Argenta Oil respect the law of Guatemala and pay farmers the compensation they rightfully owe.* Then gather signatures.

Or carry things further and mount a demonstration.

Just a few ideas.

In justice,

Jamaica

P.S. There's strength—and fun—in numbers: band with friends!

P.S.S. Speaking of fun: instead of being *against*, what can you be *for*?

From: LittleLizaJane@whoohoo.com
To: OilWatch@geemail.com

Dear Jamaica,
Thanks for the exciting ideas.

My friends and I have formed GRRR!—Girls for Renewable Resources, Really! We've already got a Facebook page, and we are writing letters to newspapers about Argenta's unpaid debt.

And—drumroll!—we're planning a demonstration at Argenta Oil's offices! We're calling it an Insistence, because we insist Argenta pays up.

GRRR! has its first official meeting this Friday.

In a hurry,

Liza

From: OilWatch@geemail.com
To: LittleLizaJane@whoohoo.com

Dear Liza!
Awesome about GRRR!

Let me know how the Insistence goes!! I'll be there in spirit! And good luck with your first meeting!

In awe,

Jamaica

Chapter Eight

The meeting is more exciting than I expected it to be. Nine girls show up— *and* three boys.

"I'm happy to see you," I tell the boys, "but it's Girls for Renewable Resources, not Girls and Boys for Renewable Resources."

"Yeah," puts in Melissa. "It's GRRR! Not GBRRR!"

"That's discribidation, Liza," Niall sniffs. He means to say *discrimination*, but his nose, as usual, is stuffed up.

I think Niall is the cutest boy in the school. He's got thick, wavy black hair down to his shoulders, big dark eyes, and this perpetual cold. If I wanted to date him, there wouldn't be much competition. He's wiry and nimble, but also permanently stooped at the shoulders from coughing so much. He only straightens out when he runs for the high jump. That's his only sport, but every year he makes the city finals.

The first time Niall ever talked to me, he told me about a pulley system he'd made. He'd nailed spools all over the walls of his room and strung them with string. I asked him what he used his pulley system for. "Nothing," he casually replied. "I just love to see the string go around and hear the spools whir and grind against the walls. It's a diagram of work." From that moment, he had my heart.

And now I'm going to tell him he can't join my group?

"Why just girls?" Harry asks.

Melissa, luckily, has an answer. "You guys will horse around. You'll take over," she says.

"Hey, that is todally unfair," Niall argues. "Stereotypes. You just want to talk your own language. And, actually, I kind of get that."

"You're worried we'll distract you," says Jarod.

"Yeah, right!" sputters Melissa, who's written Jarod's name at least six hundred times on her binder, with the *o* in the shape of a heart.

Luckily, Harry gets a brainwave. "Hey, guys! How about BRRR!? That would be cool—or cold. Boys for Renewable Resources, Really! The Earth's heating up, but BRRR! cools it down. Wind and solar power all the way!"

"Yeah!" I cheer. "We could be sister organizations. I mean sibling organizations."

"I've already got a project we could do!" Niall cries. "A bike rodeo to raise money for solar panels for the school roof. For hot water."

"Great idea!" Jarod high-fives Niall. As well as being extremely good-looking, Jarod is also the winner of the Golden Shoe Award every year. He bikes to and from school no matter how dark and rainy it is. "Then we'll get Victoria to capture the energy from the storm drains. Direct the water into a turbine and have it power the city's streetlights! Water's heavy and powerful!"

The guys put their arms around each other and head up the hall chanting, "Water's heavy. Water's powerful. The sun's strong. The sun's superior."

We decide to hold our Insistence, otherwise known as a protest, on the next Pro-D day.

Myra is going to collect email addresses for local TV and radio stations, and newspapers and magazines. Janine and Emma T. will write the media release that we'll send to all of them. Melissa is going to call City Hall to find out if we need a permit. I am going to make three dozen mini air horns for the demo.

Janine has the great idea of putting a photograph of the president of Argenta Oil's house next to a photo of a Mayan home on the press release. What a great way to show who's getting rich. I volunteered Olive to research where he lives.

We set a date for a sign-making party. I am elected "chair" of the event, which means I'll do the interviews with media.

We consider a silent protest. Every Friday afternoon, a group of women stand silently at a downtown corner with signs against war. "Women in Black" they call themselves. They dress in black to honor the people who've died in wars. In the end we decide against silence. GRRR! is going to be loud.

I bike the long way home. The winter air is delicious; even the soggy leaves in the gutter smell rich! I'm totally excited about GRRR! Heck, I'm even excited about BRRR! But my heart sinks when Slick's SUV is in front of our house.

He is over for supper, *again*. He has brought ten packages of sushi.

"Isn't that a lot for five people?" I ask as I put my books on the dishwasher.

"Well, I ran ten kilometers this afternoon, so I'm pretty hungry," Slick answers. He's boasting, as usual.

"Robert's in the Run for the Cure on Sunday," Mom explains.

"Run for the what?" Silas asks as he peels the seaweed off his sushi.

He won't eat green food, not even green jujubes.

"It's a fundraiser for research, for breast cancer," says Mom.

"Isn't that the run that made you so mad last year?" I ask. "Yeah, you told us it should be called Run for Prevention."

Mom looked uncomfortable. "Uh, yeah, I think so."

"You said money would be better spent banning pesticides or toxic cleaning products. You said Run for the Cure raises money for labs that test on animals." I want Slick to hear how Mom really feels—and Mom knows it.

She rubs her forehead. "Yes, I did say that," she sighs. "But, you know, I really don't have all the information."

"Mom! Are you taking it back?" I demand.

A flash of anger crosses Mom's face. She looks me in the eyes. I hold her stare. Silas and Leland look from me to her, from her to me. Finally Mom's face softens.

"You're right, Liza Jane. No, I'm not taking back what I said," she says.

"I'd be interested to know if they do test on animals," Slick speaks up. "That's something I've never agreed with. I had a pet mouse when I was a boy and can sincerely say he was my friend."

Then he clears the empty sushi trays from the table and dumps them in the garbage. I give Mom a look.

Mom straightens her shoulders. "Robert?" she says. "If you don't mind, there's a blue box under the sink. Those containers can be recycled."

"They *can*?" Slick asks, genuinely amazed.

"Yeah," says Mom. "And, um, I've been meaning to say, it's actually against the law in Victoria to throw paper in the garbage."

Robert just stands in the middle of our kitchen looking stunned.

"And SUVs should be illegal too," I mutter. Mom gives me a warning look.

"I see," Slick drawls, nodding. "Do you ever feel like you've been on holiday and missed something?" He rinses the containers and drops them into the blue box. The noise of him clattering around is a victory symphony.

Chapter Nine

Plans for the Insistence are ticking along.
There's only one problem: Olive. She
joined GRRR! but refuses to protest. The
day of our sign-making party, she comes
over early to tell me. She says the protest
is illegal.

Melissa contacted the City's bylaw
office, I tell her, and found out we're
totally legal as long as we don't block

traffic and stay off private property. We've decided to wave our signs in the small park in front of Argenta's offices. "It's legal as a beagle," I say. "Legal as a seagull. As a bagel."

"Okay." Olive smiles. "But I don't have the same days off as you." Olive goes to private school.

"You can miss a morning," I argue. "You take time off for swim competitions."

But Olive isn't listening. In fact, she looks like she's going to cry. "What is it *really*, Olive?" I ask.

Olive looks out my window toward home. "I've got to go. My laundry's in the dryer. I've got to fold it and put it away." I know this is an excuse. What is Olive hiding from me?

"Your heart's a pocket!" I sing. Olive laughs. Her dad taped this nerdy poem to her wall: *Your heart's a pocket. Not a locket. Reach inside, and talk it, talk it.*

"Okay." Olive gulped. "I'm scared. I don't know why, but that's what I feel. *Deep down in my pocket!*" Olive rolls her eyes. But I can tell she feels lighter.

"Well, is Argenta Oil in the wrong?" I ask.

"Yes. I know they are."

"Do you want to ask them to pay up?"

"I do. But a protest seems so…rude. You're making them look bad."

"They're *being* bad," I say. "Olive, the farmers have tried the nice way for *two years*."

Olive starts to cry. She often cries when we argue. She thinks it's the end of our friendship. Olive and her family never argue. If Olive raises her voice, she's sent to her room.

It's a different story with my family. "Arguing unblocks the vents," Mom says. "It cleans the whistle, shakes the sand out of your trousers." Mom thinks if you *don't* let your anger out, you get an ulcer.

I put my arms around Olive. "I know you hate arguing," I say. She goes stiff. She doesn't get a lot of hugging practice at home either. "But if the company gets angry, it's because *they've* been embarrassed by their own bad behavior. But do what you're comfortable with, Olive. Follow your gut."

Olive eyes the stack of wood we begged from workers tearing down a house on the next block. "I'll think about it some more," she says, wiping her eyes. "By the way," she says with a wink, "Mr. President, Gavin Helsop, lives at 2226 West Rochester Terrace."

I'm amazed. "How did you get his address so quickly?"

"It's in the phone book," Olive replies.

"Duh!" we both say and laugh.

The doorbell rings. The girls of GRRR! are arriving.

Mom is at an auction, so we don't have to sneak around. We push my bed against the wall to make space to work. We laugh a lot as we compose slogans.

"How about 'Argenta Sucks'?" Melissa suggests.

"That's too disrespectful," says Emma. "People won't respect us if we're rude." Emma walks a fine line between good judgment and goody-goody. But we agree that our slogans should be respectful.

We do our signs in black paint on green poster board. The black paint is supposed to symbolize the ugly oil ruining the Earth.

"Keep your messages short, then your letters can be big, easier to read," I remind everyone.

Silas and Leland staple the cardboard to the sticks, then the posters over top.

We make twenty signs. *Pay Up. Argenta Owes $$$. Hand Over Your Bonus. Settle Your Debts. Two Years*

Too Long! We also compose chants:
"Oh Ho! Hey Hey! Argenta Oil has got
to pay!" "Broken fences, ruined roads.
Pay the Maya what you owe!" "If you
drill, pay the bill!"

Finally we write to the tune of
"Miss Mary Mack":

Argenta Oil, Oil, Oil
Is much too spoiled, spoiled, spoiled
to pay the bills, bills, bills,
for where it drills, drills, drills.
Drink cappuccino, -ccino, -ccino
while the *campesino*, -sino, -sino
cries for her land, land, land,
can't understand, -stand,-stand.
Put down your cup, cup, cup
you've had enough, enough, enough.
The Earth's your ma, ma, ma—
obey the law, law, law!

The ten of us are singing, clapping
and laughing in a mess of tape, scissors,

markers and staplers when Mom appears at the door.

"What on *earth*? What is going on? Liza?" Our eyes meet. She's angry.

"You said I could have some friends over—," I sputter.

"I didn't imagine *this* many, Liza Jane. Girls, I'm happy to see you, but—" Mom reads Emma's sign. "'Argenta Owes?' You mean Argenta Oil? Liza, could you please come into the living room?"

The girls of GRRR! send me sympathetic looks. But I'm not worried. We aren't doing anything wrong.

"We're holding a protest outside of Argenta's offices," I blurt once I'm in the living room.

Mom says nothing at first. I can tell her thoughts are racing. She squints, then scowls, then chews her bottom lip, then goes calm and smiles at me. Then she starts squinting again. I wait for the next smile, and then I start in.

"I couldn't have told you because you would have told Slick—I mean, your boyfriend—and that would ruin it."

"When are you doing this thing?"

"Next Friday. It's a Pro-D day."

"But why a protest? Why don't you write letters, circulate a petition—"

"Mom, that's been done. Lawyers have written letters for two years. They don't get an answer."

"A letter isn't really your style, Liza, I admit that." Mom smiles. "It's just, well, it's awkward, with Robert being my—"

"Fine!" I say. Why had Mom gone so wobbly? "The Maya can drink from poisoned wells!"

"Whoa, Liza. It's just that, in families, we need to respect each other, support each other."

"Slick isn't part of our family, Mom," I say.

"Well, he's pretty close. Anyway, it isn't fair to embarrass friends."

"I'm not embarrassing *him*, Mom. This is about Argenta Oil. There's no sign saying *Robert is Scum*."

"Liza!"

"I've thought about this, Mom, I really have. I'm not out to get Robert. Argenta owes money, and they've got lots to spare. They think no one will notice because Guatemala's far away. Well, we're bringing Guatemala to their front door. Hey! Good idea. I wonder if it's too late to get some dirt from Guatemala shipped up. That would be cool!"

"You wouldn't have time," Mom says. "Soil is live. You can't transport live things across the border without a period in quarantine. But it is a good idea." Mom smiles. Then she looks me gently in the eyes. "Sweetie, I can't keep this a secret from Robert."

"But that will ruin the protest, Mom!" I say. "He'll tell, and they'll close the office for the day. We want everyone in that building to know that their employer won't clean up its own crap."

"Watch your language!" Mom scolds. Her face starts its contortions of thought again. Then she calms. "Liza, I'm really very proud of you. You got all these girls together, you've planned an event, you're speaking out against injustice—"

She looks dreamily out the window. "Maybe I should join Voice of Women for Peace again," she wonders aloud. "Or WILPF."

"WILPF?" I ask. I jump onto the couch and start barking: "*Wilpf! Wilpf!*"

"Women's International League for Peace and Freedom, silly!" Mom laughs. She heads up the stairs to her office. "I'll just check out their website, see what they're up to after all these years."

"So, Mom?" I call. "Are you going to tell him or not?"

"What? Oh. Liza, I can only promise that the company won't know ahead of time."

That would have to be good enough.

FOR IMMEDIATE RELEASE

Friday, November 16, 2010

Attn. Media: Victoria Girls Demand that Argenta Oil Respect the Law:

(Victoria, BC)

Kids may have the day off school, but there's no day off for justice.

GRRR!—Girls for Renewable Resources, Really!—will surprise Argenta Oil today with a rally at 10:00 AM.

Argenta Oil owes fifty Guatemalan families half a million dollars for damage caused by drilling on their land. For two years Mayan coffee farmers of the Ixcán region have asked Argenta Oil to pay up, as required by Guatemalan law. The farmers, with the support of the US group OilWatch, recently launched a court case, which they can't afford. Meanwhile, the CEO of Argenta received a $2 million bonus last year.

GRRR! wants Argenta Oil to do the right thing and pay what they owe.

This is GRRR!'s first protest. They expect a crowd of fifty.

For more information, contact Liza Maybird at LittleLizaJane@whoohoo.com

From: LittleLizaJane@whoohoo.com
To: OilWatch@geemail.com

Jamaica!!!
I feel like a weary soldier returned from—yes—a victorious campaign! We won!

The Insistence, in detail:

7:00 AM: Melissa sends press releases from her mom's fax machine.

9:50 AM: The girls of GRRR! (minus my friend Olive) arrive at Argenta offices with thirty-six signs, a goldfish bowl for donations, pamphlets, and copies of my essay about oil exploration in Guatemala (I got an A+!).

9:55 AM: I despair. It's a scrawny crowd: only six of us and a few parents. But then— wow!—girls start arriving from all directions, on bike, foot, in groups, solo. Our emails and texts and Facebook page got the word out! Next come the newspaper reporters, radio people with microphones, TV crews with cameras.

10:00 AM: We raise our signs. People start blowing on their mini air horns. That gets us plenty of attention. I turn on the bullhorn Jennifer brought and start the chants. Workers inside the building rush to the windows. Most of them look confused, some angry, some thoughtful.

10:10 AM: Two security guards exit the building. One's big and angry. The other smiles at me and winks.

10:15 AM: A worker yells, "Get a job!" and another shouts, "Go away."

Our fishbowl is filling with coins and bills. Total strangers join us. A worker on the third floor gives a thumbs-up through the window.

Slick, my mother's boyfriend, is nowhere to be seen.

10:20 AM: Olive walks up, which is very cool because she had said she wouldn't join the protest. She grabs a sign and hands me a bunch of papers. It's a petition. Nearly every girl in her school signed. There are four hundred signatures. The friendly security guard nudges me. "I'll take that up to *el presidente*," he says, heading inside.

10:25 AM: The front door opens, and a man in a business suit exits, flanked by security guards. His mouth keeps opening and closing, fishlike. Of course, it's Gavin Helsop, the president; I know his face from the website.

Helsop raises his hands. The crowd silences. I offer the bullhorn. He looks at it as if it's covered in H1N1, but takes it.

He tries to tell the crowd it's just a misunderstanding, but everyone boos and yells.

Helsop's hands are trembling! I actually feel sorry for him. But then I see his gleaming gold cufflinks.

Everyone starts chanting, "Pay up! Pay up!"

Helsop backs toward the building. Maybe he realizes how sneaky he looks slinking away, or maybe he actually sees the light, because suddenly he looks calmly at the sky and raises the bullhorn to his lips.

"Compensation will be paid by the end of the month," he says. "You have my word."

Joy! For ten minutes we scream and jump and laugh and hug. I did interviews for an hour. There's going to be lots of press. No way will Argenta be able to go back on their word!

From: OilWatch@geemail.com
To: LittleLizaJane@whoohoo.com

Liza!

Awesome! Way to go, girl!

You'll be hearing from some very happy Guatemalans. I called them today.

Peace and jubilation,

Jamaica

P.S. My twelve-year-old daughter Libby—for Liberty—is starting a Seattle chapter of GRRR!

From: AbogadaJusta@caliente.com
To: LittleLizaJane@whoohoo.com

Hola!

My name is Isabela Cardoza. I'm a lawyer in Guatemala working on behalf of the fifty families awaiting compensation. I would like to thank you very, very much for your wonderful work in Canada. Gracias! If ever you are in

Guatemala, please visit—I have a ten-year-old daughter who would love to meet a Canadian hero.

From: LaGenteUnida@nacion.com
To: LittleLizaJane@whoohoo.com

Senorita Liza Maybird,
Our hearts are full of thanks. We have worked a long time to get the oil company to listen. But you got good and close to their ears!

We will be thinking of you at the *fiesta* tonight as we dance to the *marimba* and eat *tamales*. We only wish you could be here too.

En solidaridad,

Los Campesinos de la Riviera Selequa

Chapter Ten

It turns out that Slick wasn't at work the morning of the protest. He was hiking up Bear Hill.

"What a day," Slick says as he sits down to dinner. "Beautiful weather. The sun always recharges me."

"So you're solar-powered?" I tease.

"I heard about your protest, Liza," Slick answers, his voice gravelly. He stares straight ahead. "On the radio, as I was driving back into town. I nearly had to pull over, I was so completely shocked."

The air in the dining room seems to go hard. None of us move. Slick glares into the distance. He seems to be thinking too. Is it possible to glare thoughtfully?

"The strange thing," he finally says, "is that I was proud of you."

Then he brings Mom's hand to his lips, and she makes that weird smile she gets when he's around. My stomach lurches. I realize there's a side of Mom that she doesn't share with me. But I'm too excited about the protest to mind.

"Kiss," Mom singsongs, then narrows her eyes challengingly.

Silas doesn't miss a beat. "Smooch."

"Peck," Leland cries out.

"Smack," I say, making a smacking sound.

"Pucker up!" Slick makes fish lips at the fish in their tank. We laugh.

"Lock lips!"
"Make out."
"Buss."
"Neck."
"French."
"Swap spit."
"Tongue."
"Ugh!"

A few weeks after the protest, Mom flies to Northern Alberta to appraise a rancher's collection of two hundred and twenty-eight boot scrapers. Yep, boot scrapers, like, to scrape mud off yer boots! The guy's oldest scraper is four hundred years old. One was once used by Canada's first prime minister, John A. Macdonald, and one was a murder weapon! Mom helped the same rancher sell a stirrup collection a few years ago.

While she's away, Slick picks me up from field-hockey practice. Here I am in the passenger seat of his roomy SUV, with GPS, iPod dock, surround sound, automatic tissue dispenser...It's weird, riding high above the other cars. I feel like we are royalty. When he stops for gas, I don't bite my tongue.

"How many kilometers do you get for a liter?" I ask.

"Seven," he answers, mumbling.

"*Seven*? We get twenty-five!"

"Yeah. Your mom's always rubbing it in."

"No kidding. You're wasting money. And spewing tons of carbon into the atmosphere."

"Your car isn't perfect. You're still spewing carbon too," he says.

"Yeah, I know. Biking is best."

Slick hands his Gold card to the jockey. He looks thoughtful, then turns to me. "Hey, why doesn't your girls' group hold a bicycle workshop? You bring your bikes, learn to oil the chain, tighten handle bars, clean brake pads…"

"We'd need someone to show us how," I say doubtfully.

"Darryl in my running club runs a bike shop. He'd do it. Maybe even for free."

"No, we'd do a trade!" Trades are totally DIY. "Ask him if he'll take five bars of all-natural soap made by me. It lasts twice as long the commercial stuff. And three cool hand-knitted toques for, say, a two-hour workshop."

"That would probably do it," Slick nods. "Darryl likes hats. He's balding."

Chapter Eleven

Two weeks later, Olive and I are up to our elbows making soap.

Olive cuts the last bar. "Hey!" she suddenly exclaims. "Isn't today the big day?"

She's right. It's the last day of November, the day Argenta's lawyers are supposed to hand over the compensation. We check my email. Sure enough, there's a letter from Jamaica. Subject line: *The Bill is Paid!!* Olive and I dance a polka around the kitchen, then read:

Dear Liza and the Girls of GRRR!

The money *in full* was wired to the campesinos' lawyers today. That's the good news.

The *bad* news is that tankers are moving in your province's coastal waters, even though they're banned. And you can expect a lot more.

A Canadian company is building a pipeline from the Alberta tar sands through your province to the ocean. Once the pipeline reaches the ocean, the oil will be shipped out to Asia and the US on supertankers.

Right now tankers are carrying thousands of liters of condensate, a flammable poisonous chemical, up your rocky coast, through Gitga'at territory. Condensate is used to thin crude oil—it's like molasses—so that it flows more easily through the pipelines.

You can bet that one day a tanker will smash against the rocky shore and spill enormous amounts of oil or condensate into the habitat of millions—no, *trillions*—of marine plants and animals.

We don't need a spill or an explosion.

Can GRRR! help raise the alarm? Oil and water don't mix!

In defiance of the oil industry,

Jamaica

"Wow," Olive whistles. "She's intense!"

"The *news* is intense, Olive!" I point out.

"Well, we've got to find out how much is true," Olive argues.

"Chickening out again?" I tease.

"No! I just want to know what's true and what isn't. And what is Gitga'at?"

The name sounds familiar. Then it hits me. "They're First Nations," I say.

"They live in Hartley Bay, in the Great Bear Rainforest, where we go every Christmas."

"Yeah, you rent that little cabin. I always wish I could go too."

"Last year Mom ordered clam chowder in the town restaurant, but they weren't serving any. The waiter told us that a big ferry had sunk nearby in 2006. It hit a huge rock and went down."

"I remember that. Two people died, right?"

"Yeah. The waiter thinks the people at the helm were having a little romance. They had turned down the lights and were playing music. A warning alarm was turned off."

"Uh, Liza, what does that have to do with clam chowder?"

"Well, the ferry has been leaking oil into the water ever since. The clam beds are badly polluted. The clams are basically poison."

Olive and I spend the rest of the afternoon researching—googling *tar sands, condensate, tankers* and *supertankers, oil spills*. The best part was learning more about the Gitga'at. Their territory is huge, way bigger than Lake Michigan. Of course, the oil companies hadn't talked with them. They just barged in, exactly like the oil companies did to the Mayans.

According to the articles we found, the Gitga'at were frightened. Some saw the ferry sinking as an omen of things to come. A supertanker is way larger than a passenger ferry.

Olive and I open Google Earth and imagine steering a supertanker, which is even bigger than a city block, down the narrow shipping route. A supertanker needs three kilometers to come to a full stop. So what if the captain and sailors are expert? The ferry operators were professionals and had the best navigating technology, but sailed straight into a giant rock sticking way up out of the water.

I am pretty angry by the time I read the comment from scientist Janie Wray, who studies whales in the area. "If there is a major oil spill, it will be the end of the Great Bear Rainforest. It would be the end of the salmon, the eagles, the bears and the wolves."

I am still mad when Slick comes over for supper. He mentions that he did some gardening that afternoon.

"Weeding?" Mom asks. "That's not fun."

"I just spray stuff from a little bottle, so it's not too hard," Slick says.

And my organic mother smiles at that! And later kisses him goodnight at the door, as usual.

"How can you kiss a guy who uses pesticides, Mom?" I ask while we wash dishes.

"I respect Robert's right to make his own choices."

"Sure, like his right to spray pesticides?" I sputter. "Do people have a right to pollute?"

"Sweetie, it's not that simple." Mom sighs. "Sure, I wish he didn't use pesticides, but I can't just tell him to stop. He's got to decide for himself."

"He's fake, fake, fake," I rage. "He bought herb sachets from the boys. What does he need with a rosemary sachet? He's trying to buy our love or something." Silas and Leland have been selling homemade sachets to raise money for a pogo stick.

"He's just trying to get to know you. And, guess what? The guy has sachets in all his clothes drawers."

"*Really*?" I ask.

"Yeah! Especially his lingerie drawer." Mom winks. I have to laugh. "I want to show you something," she says, firing up her laptop to YouTube.

She shows me a video. An artist in Sweden has turned a set of stairs in a subway station into a giant piano. When someone steps on a stair, a note rings out. It is so fun, everyone starts using the stairs instead of the escalator beside it.

"You catch more flies with honey than with vinegar," Mom says. "People don't listen to things that make them feel bad. They hear the people who make them laugh."

"Like the basketball hoop you put over the laundry basket," I say. "Way more fun to shoot dirty socks through the hoop than drop them on the floor."

"Yeah. Make it fun, make it easy, make it irresistible," Mom chanted. "Rather than gripe, 'Don't Spray Pesticides,' how about you sing, 'Garden with Soul'?"

"I get it," I say. "Still, you have to speak up when something's wrong. Ms. Catalla says if you don't, you're part of the problem."

"You need to speak up, yes. But be patient, choose the right time. In the meantime, show by example."

"How do you know all this, Mom?"

"I've rocked the boat a little in my time," she says. "But mostly I learned it by being a mother."

Chapter Twelve

Twenty-four girls—with twenty-four bikes—show up for Girls on Wheels. Luckily, Darryl has lots of tools. He's funny and keeps us laughing. Tuning up our bikes is a breeze. We timed the workshop for the last Friday of the month, so afterward we head out for a "critical mass" ride. Every month, thousands of cyclists in over three hundred cities join up to pedal around town, filling the streets with a healthy vibe. This time, GRRR! is among them. Darryl leads.

"Pedal Power All the Way!" we yell. "No emissions! No noise! No roadkill!" And, "Whose streets? Our streets!"

It's exhilarating! Plenty of cars honk—some to cheer us on, others to curse us.

"We're traffic too!" we answer. It isn't until we get to the Legislature grounds and stop to say our goodbyes that I realize how cold it is. December is around the corner.

"That was the best!" Olive exclaims.

"You're positively rosy!" I tell her.

"I want to do it again next month!" she cries.

But as we ride home, she quiets. "My parents won't like it," she says. "They'll say it's dangerous, or too public."

"Olive, it's a bike ride," I say soothingly. "How can that be bad?"

"You're right. Just a bike ride. That's what I'll say."

We stop at the corner to say goodbye.

"That was great of your mom's boyfriend to organize the workshop," Olive enthuses.

"Whatever," I say. "He just wants me on his side. He's buying me off so he can have my mom."

"When my parents and I moved into the neighborhood, you baked us a blackberry crumble," Olive says. "Were you just trying to buy us?"

"I was being friendly. You know that. Neighborly."

"So maybe Robert's being neighborly."

"Yeah, well, I don't want him in the neighborhood."

"Liza Maybird, it sounds like *you're* the one with the problem. Not him."

I feel myself turn red. I want to hide. I want to scream and say it isn't true.

"You sure are good at fixing your bike," Olive says then, raising her eyebrows thoughtfully. And I know what she's trying to say. She's saying that she sees the real me, whether I'm being smart, like when I'm fixing my bike, or whether I'm being stupid.

At supper, Mom drops a little bomb. "This Christmas, I'd like Robert to come to the Great Bear Rainforest with us." She watches us nervously.

I feel like my breath has been sucked out of me. I want to leave the room.

"Yippee!" the boys start screaming. But when they see my face, they quiet down.

"We all know that Liza isn't fond of Robert, so this isn't exciting news for her," Mom says gently.

"It's lousy news," I yell, bursting into tears. "The worst!" I run from the room.

Minutes later, Leland visits me. I'm facedown on my bed, sobbing. "Cake for 'Iza?" Leland asks, holding out a plate of chocolate cake. He calls me 'Iza as a pet name. It's how he said my name when he was a baby.

"Thanks, Lee-Lee, I'm not hungry."

Silas comes in with a mug of mint tea. "Thanks," I say, sitting up. "You really like that guy, eh?" I ask them.

"Yeah, he's fun. Not as fun as Dad," Silas says. "But Dad's far away."

"The tea's good. Thanks," I say.

"I put extra honey in it for you," Silas says.

Mom finally comes in and sits on the edge of my bed. "Sweetie, tell me what you're feeling."

"Mad," I blubber. "He's always in our lives now. Here for supper, at the boys' soccer games, at parties. Whenever you get a free moment, you're on the phone with him, or getting your hair done for him. I never see you, just *you*, anymore. It's never just *us*. He comes first, and we just get pushed aside for him. You drive up to his house, and I get in the backseat! It sucks!"

I don't think. I just talk. And Mom doesn't argue. She doesn't interrupt to say it isn't that bad or that I'm just tired. She's really listening. Finally I'm talked out, and Mom's sitting there, crying a little and nodding. The boys are spellbound.

At last, Mom speaks. "Liza, I am so proud of you for telling me how you feel. I understand. And I'm sorry. I was so excited about meeting someone who makes me laugh and feel good, that I jumped in quickly. And left you guys on the shore sometimes.

"How about this: how about Robert just comes up to Great Bear for two nights. We're there for a whole week. Would that be acceptable?"

"I'd rather not see him at all," I pout.

"Okay, then, three nights," Mom says, cracking a smile.

"Two!" I laugh. "I can handle him for two."

Silas and Leland start whooping then and jumping on my bed. After a bit, Mom and I join in—until the bed makes an evil-sounding crack. We freeze and then fall into a giggling heap.

FOR IMMEDIATE RELEASE
Friday, December 10, 2010

<u>Attn. Media: Keep Our Coast Tanker-Free</u>
(Victoria, BC)

GRRR! is at it again. On Friday at Arbutus Beach, under a full moon, Girls for Renewable Resources, Really! will set afloat three hundred origami boats. The seaweed-paper boats represent the three hundred tankers that may soon travel our coast each year—at our peril.

If the oil industry gets its way, enormous tankers filled with oil from the Alberta tar sands will travel our rocky coast in all kinds of weather, through the territory of the Gitga'at, past the exact place where the BC Ferry *Queen of the North* smashed into Gil Rock.

An oil spill is inevitable. It will kill plankton, salmon, otters, whales, seabirds and also the wolves and bears on shore that feed on salmon.

Already, tankers of condensate travel our coast for use at the Alberta tar sands.

Join us in solemn recognition and joyful celebration of the four elements—air, fire, earth and WATER.

GRRR! will be joined by BRRR!—Boys for Renewable Resources, Really!—and at the exact same time, in Seattle, a sister chapter of GRRR! will also launch boats.

Chapter Thirteen

Mom is at an auction, so Slick picks me and the boys up from soccer. It is eleven o'clock on a freezing Saturday morning in December, but he takes us out for ice cream!

"Cool!" Leland says when Slick pulls into Beacon Drive In.

"More like 'cold!'" Silas jokes.

"Br-r-right idea!" I say, making an effort to join in. Slick brought four golf putters and we play mini-golf in Beacon Hill Park. A squirrel and a crow fight over the last of our cones, and Slick shows Leland how to make a whistle from a blade of grass. Slick sucks at golf.

"I've tried," he says. "It's how the oil bosses hobnob. But I just can't get it."

"Golf courses are weird," I comment. "Giant lawns with holes."

"A dead dreamland," Leland says.

We go to Slick's house for lunch. "I've got a surprise for you," he says. In his backyard, he's hung three handmade swings from his Garry oak trees. Our names are painted on them in swirling letters. Mine is a beautiful curved piece of arbutus.

"Reclaimed wood," Slick said. "I scavenged it. Loggers leave a lot behind."

"I didn't know you could—," I started.

"Make things?" Slick smiles. "I grew up on a farm. We were very poor. We did everything ourselves. I didn't have a piece of clothing that wasn't a hand-me-down until I was fourteen. A white Oxford shirt, for my first job."

"What was it?" asked Silas. "Your first job?"

"Gofer."

"*What?*" we chorus.

"Go for this, go for that. Errand boy, in a field office of the very company I work for today. Argenta Oil has been my bread and butter since I was fourteen."

"Butter?" I asked. "Don't you mean oil?"

"Get out of here, you!" Slick laughs. "Let me make lunch."

We swing high in the backyard while Slick makes peanut-butter sandwiches. We eat outside, wrapped in blankets.

"Nothing like a picnic," Slick sighs. Leland plucks a piece of grass from the yard and puts it to his lips.

"Don't!" Slick cries. "It's been sprayed."

"Pesticides," I say.

"You mean—" Leland looks bewildered. "You poison your own lawn?"

Slick is at a loss for words. "That reminds me!" I leap in, reaching into my jacket pocket. "I printed this off for you! It's from the Canadian Cancer Society website. You know, the organization you did that run for? They want Canada to ban the use of pesticides for 'cosmetic reasons'—like making lawns and parks, *and* golf courses, pretty. Pesticides can make kids get leukemia."

But I was supposed to make the message fun, right? "And, uh, guess what? For Christmas, I'm giving you four hours of weeding by *moi*."

Slick is reading and shaking his head. Finally he looks up. "Four hours of weeding sounds like an excellent gift," he said. "Thank you."

Holy cow. I just gave Slick, my hated enemy, a Christmas present.

What is getting into me?

Later that night, Olive arrives at the GRRR! boat-folding meeting early, tearful and livid.

"Why did you post those photos of the bike ride on your Facebook page?" she hisses at me. "Did you forget my parents are your Facebook friends?"

"Yeah," I stammer. "Kind of. I mean, I wasn't worried about who would see them."

"They saw we were riding in the middle of the street. You *knew* I wasn't going to tell them the whole story! I'm grounded," she fumes. "I can't go to the flotilla launch."

"Wow. That *really* sucks," I say. "Is there any way you can change their minds? Do more chores or something?"

"No. They think I'm in over my head, that I'm going with the crowd because I'm not 'centered.'"

"That's what you get when your dad's a psychiatrist," I say, half-smiling, half-commiserating.

"At least I can help fold boats." Olive sighs. "Let's get to it."

Chapter Fourteen

On Sunday evening, Leland, Silas and I are the first to arrive at Arbutus Beach. Mom drops us off with the box of paper boats and heads out for a coffee with Slick. It's a cold, clear night. The moon is a bright coin in the black sky. The beach glows silver, and the waves seem to lap at the moonlight. To keep warm, the boys and I run along the logs on shore. Suddenly we hear a splash. Out in the dark ocean we spy the glistening wet head of a seal. She seems to see us too, then disappears beneath the water. Finally she bobs up again in a different spot, looks at us and disappears again.

"It's like she's sewing. Up and down," Leland remarks.

Silas agrees. "Like she's lashing together the underwater world and our world above."

"Do you think she knows we're here, Liza? What we're doing?" Leland asks.

"I do think she knows," I muse. "Even if she doesn't know she knows."

"I kind of get that," says Silas.

"Me too," Leland says. "It makes me shivery. Magic shivery."

We squat side by side and wait for the seal to pop up again. I realize that my arms are over my brothers' shoulders.

"I'm warm," says Silas.

"Me too," I say.

"Me three," Leland chimes in.

Then a man's voice rises cheerfully behind us. "Is this the launch site for three hundred boats?" It's Darryl, and about twelve others! "My soccer team," Darryl explains, slightly out of breath. "We just finished a game."

The beach soon gets busy. The girls from GRRR! arrive, other kids from school, their parents, and even Ms. Catalla! Our babysitter Rachael arrives with four friends from music school. They have violins and violas and begin playing.

"*Water Music* by Handel," Rachael announces.

Melissa, Emma and I hand out boats. Even the news reporters take them. The boys of BRRR! arrive with Mr. McCartney in tow. "I like your boat design," Niall tells me shyly. "Sturdy, but elegant." He gives me a strange smile.

I smile back, but my lips do something weird—they kind of quiver.

Melissa grabs my elbow. "Make your speech!" she whispers.

With his booming voice, Darryl calls for the crowd's attention. The wind dies down right at that moment, so I don't have to shout.

"There are environmentally gentle boats," I begin, reading the speech I've worked on for a week, "such as the Salish dugout canoes that traveled these waters for thousands of years. And there are aggressive boats, such as motorboats and container ships. Our coast is wild and rough. It is also sensitive and complex as lace. Plankton, seaweed, salmon, seals, eagles—just as *we* need clean water, they do too.

"We can't let tankers bully up and down our narrow inlets. Yes, the oil they carry means a kind of life—movement and money. But it takes only a drop of oil the size of a dime to kill a seagull. Imagine a sleepy captain, hurricane-force winds, a broken computer. And a tanker loses its way and crashes, spilling hundreds of thousands of gallons of oil.

"The boats we're sending out this evening are gentle boats. They won't hurt the ocean and its creatures. They're at home here. Tankers are not. Ready? Launch!"

At first the boats cling to shore. A few nervous laughs. But Hannah's mom, a kayaker, says the currents at Arbutus will soon carry the boats off. And they do, as if stirred by a witch's wand.

"Wonderful speech, daughter."

I wheel around. It's Mom! "What are you doing here? And—Ro-Robert. Hello."

"Surprise!" Slick grins. He's got a boat in his hand. "Launch time, Laura." I can't believe it. I look around at the crowd—they sure have no idea an oil executive is among them!

Mom launches her boat while Slick removes his fancy shoes. I guess he doesn't want to get them wet. Mom comes over and puts her arms around me. We watch as Slick crouches at the water's edge and gives his boat a little push.

"Robert's been learning from you," Mom says quietly. "He says you walk the talk."

Robert joins us. "This is really beautiful, Liza," he says. Then he looks me in the eye. "I know it's a bit weird that I'm here. But I want to take your message to the company."

"Robert's going to research his company's records," Mom says.

"I've been very thankful to the company. They've given me a living," Robert explains. "But maybe I've been too thankful. I just assumed they were doing the right thing. When I learned they were dragging their feet on those compensation payments, I was shocked.

"Now, I want to make sure the company doesn't step on the Gitga'at. Or endanger the environment. I'm going to be asking hard questions at meetings over the next few weeks."

"Just taking oil out of the ground is bad for the environment," I say. "And for what? For rich people to burn up in their Hummers?"

"Liza—," Mom warns.

"She has a point," Slick says. "And it's a good one."

"Anyway, couldn't you lose your job?" I ask.

"It's possible," Slick nods and looks out at the water. "Does GRRR! have an opening for a CEO?"

"No!" I laugh.

Slick nods. "You know, I like my job. And the pay is nice. But you and your mom and your brothers, you bring me a lot of happiness. You make me rich, the real kind of rich."

So maybe Slick isn't such a bad guy, I'm thinking. He acts on what he learns. *That's* cool. Maybe he's like a rattleback. Maybe he will switch directions completely.

The crowd starts to thin. People head home. The three hundred paper boats bob in the moonlight. Overnight, they'll dissolve into the water.

The girls of GRRR! huddle with our heads together:

"Way to go," Melissa enthuses.

"Beautiful," Emma T. concurs.

"Here's to happy salmon!" I say.

"To green forests!"

"To blue waters."

"To Olive, who wanted to be here."

"Hip hip, hooray!" we hug each other.

Then Mom, Silas, Leland and I— and Slick—pile into the car. "Wait!"

Slick shouts as I climb into the back. "My turn."

He takes my arm and leads me to the front seat. Then *he* gets in between Silas and Leland. "Enjoy the ride, everyone," Mom says. "We're getting on our bikes tomorrow. Time to walk the talk."

"You mean bike the gripe," Silas jokes.

I look at the backseat. Silas is rosy-cheeked from the night air. Leland is dozing off. And Slick just looks squashed, his knees practically pressed into his eye sockets.

Mom squeezes my knee and smiles. "Homeward, co-pilot?" she asks.

"Homeward," I reply.

The cuffs of my jeans are wet with sea water. They're rough and cold against my ankles. But I don't mind. I don't mind at all.

Epilogue

From: OilWatch@geemail.com
To: LittleLizaJane@whoohoo.com

Comrade Liza!
Attached are photos of the Seattle GRRR!
flotilla. A beautiful night.

I got a letter from the farmers of the Riviera
Selequa. Oil spills have polluted lands along a
pipeline that crosses thousands of hectares
of indigenous land. The government and oil

companies say it isn't their fault. They're threatening to jail environmentalists, journalists and local leaders who try to speak out.

They want me to let you know.

Rise up!

Jamaica

From: OliveJuice@lalaland.ca
To: LittleLizaJane@whoohoo.com

Liza!

Ran into Niall, and he gushed about your amazing speech.

While you were on the beach, I got my parents to watch *An Inconvenient Truth*, that movie about climate change. It was like watching two people turn into rocks. They went dead silent. Then we had a family meeting. We've turned down the heat in the house three degrees—I need slippers—and we're not buying anything new except food for a year! You just might see me at the next Critical Mass ride!

Love, Olive Pit

From: aLynne@gitga'at.com
To: LittleLizaJane@whoohoo.com

Dear Liza,

I read about your flotilla launch in the newspaper. Wonderful!

I live on the Douglas Channel.

Sometimes people block roads so logging
trucks can't get through and wreck the
wilderness.

You can't block water as easily. So I
dream of crocheting a chain of wool and
stretching it across the Channel. The little
string wouldn't stop the tankers, but it would
symbolize the fragility of our existence and
show the magnitude of our fight.

Would GRRR! be interested in doing a
little crocheting?

Sincerely,

Lynne Hill

Author's Note

While most of *Slick* is fictional, much is true. The Maya people's land and human rights are continually violated by the oil industry, especially the Maya Queqchi people, who live in a central strip of Guatemala.

Oil spills have polluted vast amounts of indigenous lands along a pipeline from a refinery in La Libertad, Peten, to Puerto Barrios, Izabal. Government officials as well as oil companies deny responsibility, and, yes, people are threatened with jail or physically hurt when they speak out.

Often indigenous peoples don't know their rights have been violated, mostly because they have long been treated as "sub-citizens" in their countries, as if they have no rights. Rich, poor, black, white— *all* people have equal human rights.

In British Columbia, since 2006, condensate tankers have traveled the

Douglas Channel and other sensitive areas, and oil supertanker traffic is a real threat. For more information, see notankers.ca.

Lynne Hill does indeed live in Hartley Bay. The crochet chain across Douglas Channel she dreams of would be four kilometers long!

Special thanks to Don and Pam. And to Mike for being a good sport. Also, to Arlette, Nicole, Mikel, Diana, Amaya, Ezra, Alden and my amazing siblings.